The Rain Forest Counts!

by Lisa McCourt

illustrated by Cheryl Nathan

BridgeWater Paperback

Published by BridgeWater Paperback, an imprint and trademark
of Troll Communications L.L.C.

First published in hardcover by BridgeWater Books.

First paperback edition published 1998.

Produced by Boingo Books, Inc.

Printed in the United States of America.

10 9 8 7 6 5 4 3

Library of Congress Cataloging-in-Publication Data

McCourt, Lisa.
The rain forest counts! / by Lisa McCourt; illustrated by Cheryl Nathan.
p.   cm.
Summary: Introduces a variety of rain forest animals while counting from one up to ten
and then back down to one again.
ISBN O-8167-4388-6 (lib. bdg.)   ISBN O-8167-4458-O (pbk.)
[1. Rain forest animals—Fiction. 2. Counting. 3. Stories in rhyme.] I. Nathan, Cheryl, 1958- ill.
II. Title.
PZ 8.3.M 13115 Rai 1997
[E]—dc 21   97-9995

To Patsy Jensen, for her relentless encouragement
—L.M.

To my mother, for her loving support
—C.N.

1 silent jaguar stalking her prey

2 scared agoutis bounding away

3 yellow crab spiders looking like flowers

4 bright bromeliads soaking up showers

5 silky anteaters hang in a hura tree

6 noisy parrots seem to disagree

7 basilisk lizards across the water run

8 woolly mouse opossums sleeping in the sun

9 heliconid butterflies in yellow, red, and black

10 hungry bush dogs hunting in a pack

9 of them are left when one turns back

8 white flowers on a tall cacao tree

7 poison dart frogs from a leimadophis flee

6 pygmy fruit bats hanging upside down

5 erolytus beetles scurry busily around

4 howler monkeys' screams echo in the night

3 harpy eagles spread their wings and take flight

2 blue-backed manakins shriek a lively chorus

1 anola lizard in the beautiful rain forest

STUFF ABOUT
THE RAIN FOREST'S PLANTS & ANIMALS

AGOUTIS are rodents about the size of large rabbits. They are very important to the rain forest because they help to plant Brazil nut trees! The fruit of the Brazil nut tree has a rock-hard outer layer. But the agouti's teeth are strong enough to crack the hard shell. Agoutis crack open the fruit to eat the nuts inside. They often bury nuts to eat later. When they forget to dig those nuts up, Brazil nut trees grow. Without agoutis, Brazil nut trees might not survive in the rain forest.

ANOLA LIZARDS are very hard to see because their skin color changes to match their surroundings. But when two male anola lizards compete for attention from a female, they're easy to spot. Each male puffs out a colorful piece of skin under his neck. Then both males open their mouths and bob their heads rapidly up and down until one lizard gives up the contest.

BASILISK LIZARDS live near water. They have fringed toes. The fringes help these lizards to travel in a way that most animals can't: When something frightens a group of basilisk lizards, they can stand on their hind legs and run straight across the top of the water!

BLUE-BACKED MANAKINS have small bodies and short wings. Their size allows them to fly in the lower layers of the rain forest, between the crowded plants and trees. When a male blue-backed manakin wants to attract a mate, he puts on an amazing show for her. Two or three males line up on a branch for their dance. Then they take turns leaping and twirling, rapidly flapping their wings and singing. Sometimes they will even clear the ground of plants or bring in special twigs to help with their shows. The leading male will end the dance with a sharp call to the others. Then he will ruffle up his red head feathers and the female will fly away with him.

BROMELIADS are a group of about two thousand plant species. The strange thing about bromeliads is that they grow right on the trunks and branches of trees. A tank bromeliad opens up like a flower, with big, strong leaves that form a bowl. Rainwater fills the bowl to make a miniature pond in a tree. Some large plants may hold up to 10 gallons (38 liters) of water. These treetop ponds become homes for worms, snails, frogs, salamanders, and crabs. Mammals and birds visit bromeliads to eat the insects living there. Monkeys drink water from the tanks. There may be as many as two hundred different kinds of organisms living in, or feeding from, a single tank bromeliad.

BUSH DOGS are very different from the dogs you see in your neighborhood. They look a little like dachshunds, with stocky bodies and short legs. But bush dogs are fierce wild animals. These powerful hunters run together in packs of up to ten dogs. They eat agoutis and other small rain forest ground-dwellers. Bush dogs love the water, and they are great swimmers and divers.

CACAO TREES give us chocolate! Small, waxy flowers grow directly on the trunk of the cacao tree. These flowers eventually become 10-inch- (25-centimeter-) long pods. People cut down the pods and split them open. Inside each pod are rows of white seeds, or beans. These beans are dried out and sent to factories, where they are roasted and ground. Then they are melted into a gooey chocolate syrup that is used to make all the kinds of chocolate you eat!

EROLYTUS BEETLES have hard front wings that cover their whole bodies and help to protect them. Underneath these hard coverings are other wings that help the beetles fly. There are about 1,900 species of brightly colored erolytus beetles, and most of them live in tropical climates like the rain forest. They live near fungus and under fungus-infested bark. That's how they got their name, which means "pleasing fungus beetle."

HARPY EAGLES are very powerful birds of prey. They stand up to 4 feet (1.2 meters) tall and eat animals as big as monkeys and sloths. Harpies need a large hunting territory to survive, so their species is especially threatened by rain forest destruction. If harpies are left in an area of rain forest that is too small to support enough prey, they will die or stop bearing young.

HELICONID BUTTERFLIES are poisonous. Their enemies know from the bright colors on their wings that these butterflies will taste bad. Many poisonous animals in the rain forest have bright colors and striking patterns. But many other species that are not poisonous have the same colors and patterns. These bright markings protect the non-poisonous animals from predators, who are fooled into thinking they are poisonous.

HOWLER MONKEYS' loud roars can be heard up to 2 miles (3.2 kilometers) away! Their howls tell other monkeys that the territory is theirs. If too many monkeys were living in the same area, they would have to fight for food and mates. With their loud cries, howler monkeys are telling other troops of monkeys, "Stay away! This area is taken!"

JAGUARS are large members of the cat family with short, golden fur and black spots. Jaguars hunt alone. They eat ground-dwelling animals like tapirs, peccaries, and agoutis. But they are also expert tree-climbers and often hunt up in the trees for sloths, lemurs, anteaters, and tree kangaroos. Jaguars are rare and beautiful. Though they can grow to be 9 feet (2.7 meters) long, it is hard to find them in the rain forest because they are very wary and their spots let them blend perfectly into the dappled, sunlit vegetation.

PARROTS can always find food in the rain forest because their heavy, hooked bills are especially suited to scooping out fruit and cracking seeds. There are more than three hundred species of parrots, and many of these stay with the same mate their whole lives. Parrots usually fly together in flocks. They are beautiful, and they can be taught to copy human speech, so they are very popular pets. For this reason, and because of rain forest destruction, many species of parrots have become endangered.

POISON DART FROGS' skin is so dangerous that native tribes have used it to coat darts and arrow tips before hunting. The "sweat" from one frog can coat as many as fifty darts. The bright colors of these frogs warn predators to stay away. A female poison dart frog will take her tiny tadpoles 100 feet (30.5 meters) or more up into the treetops and place them in a bromeliad for safety. She'll come back once a day to feed them with one of her own unfertilized eggs. The snake, *Leimadophis*, is immune to the poison of certain poison dart frogs.

PYGMY FRUIT BATS are so small and light, they can easily hang upside down from a leaf. Over half the mammals in the rain forest are bats, and many are fruit-eaters. These bats help trees to continue growing in the rain forest. A bat will take its fruit to a safe perch, suck out the juice, and throw away the seeds. Some very small seeds will be eaten and passed out in the bat's droppings as it flies over the forest. In this way, bats spread the seeds that keep new trees growing. Fruit bats in African and Indian forests are hunted for their meat. This causes species of bats *and* trees to become endangered.

SILKY ANTEATERS are named for their soft, silky fur. They have no teeth, but their sharp claws help them find ants, and their sticky tongues are perfect for catching and eating them. Silky anteaters are only 18 inches (46 centimeters) long. They hang from their tails in the treetops, searching for termites and ants. These silky anteaters are hanging in a *hura tree*. Hura trees can grow to be 130 feet (39.6 meters) tall and live for over one hundred years.

WOOLLY MOUSE OPOSSUMS sleep all day and hunt at night. When they are frightened by another animal, they will "play possum," pretending to be dead so that the other animal will leave them alone. Opossums have pouches where they carry their babies, just like kangaroos.

YELLOW CRAB SPIDERS are tricky hunters. When this spider sits on a leaf, it looks like a common rain forest flower that has fallen from a tree. All the spider has to do is wait for an unsuspecting fly or bee to come visit the phony flower. Then the spider blows its disguise as it catches a tasty meal!